The Adventures of BERT

Allan Ahlberg & Raymond Briggs

Farrar, Straus and Giroux • New York

Library of Congress catalog card number: 2001 132002
Printed in Italy
First published in Great Britain by Viking Books, 2001
First American edition, 2001
1 3 5 7 9 10 8 6 4 2

CHAPTER ONE

Bert

B

Meet Bert.
This is him.
Say hallo to Bert.

Meet Mrs. Bert.
This is her.
Say hallo to her
as well.

Meet Baby Bert.
Don't say hallo to him.
He is fast asleep.

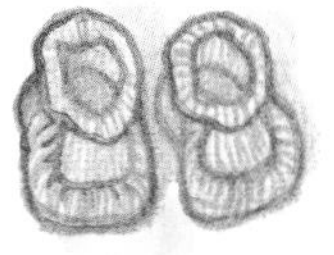

Shh!
Turn the page . . . quietly.

Oh no!
Now look what you've done.

CHAPTER TWO

Bert and the Shirt

One day, Bert has
an adventure with a shirt.

Here is the shirt.
Do you like it?

Bert puts
the shirt on.
It gets stuck
over his head.

He falls downstairs.

He rolls into the street.

He rolls into a truck.

He ends up in Scotland.

Poor Bert!

CHAPTER THREE

Bert and the Sausage

The next day, Bert has
an adventure with a sausage.

Bert is out shopping.
He sees a sausage on the street.

Bert runs off.

The sausage chases him.

Bert falls over.

Bert bangs his nose.

But it is only a man in a sausage suit,
selling sausages.
The sausage man helps Bert to his feet.
He gives him his hat back
. . . and a free sausage.

Lucky Bert!

CHAPTER FOUR

Bert and the Cardboard Box

The *next* day, Bert has
an adventure with a cardboard box.

Bert is walking by the river.
He sees a cardboard box go floating by.
There it is—look!

The box is big and brown
. . . and *barking*.

Bert dives in
to rescue the box.

Then he remembers—
he can't swim.

Bert splashes!

Bert shouts!

Bert sinks!

Bert . . . stands up.

The water is not as deep as he thought.

Bert lies on the bank.

A *puppy* creeps out of the box.

He licks Bert's face.

Bert is his hero.

Brave Bert!

CHAPTER FIVE

Good night, Bert!

It is bedtime now.
Bert is in his pajamas.
Say good night to Bert.

Mrs. Bert is in her pajamas.
Say good night to her as well.

Baby Bert
is in his crib.
Don't say good night
to him.
Don't make a sound.

Shh!
Turn the page
very, very. . . quietly.

Oh no!
You’ve done it again!

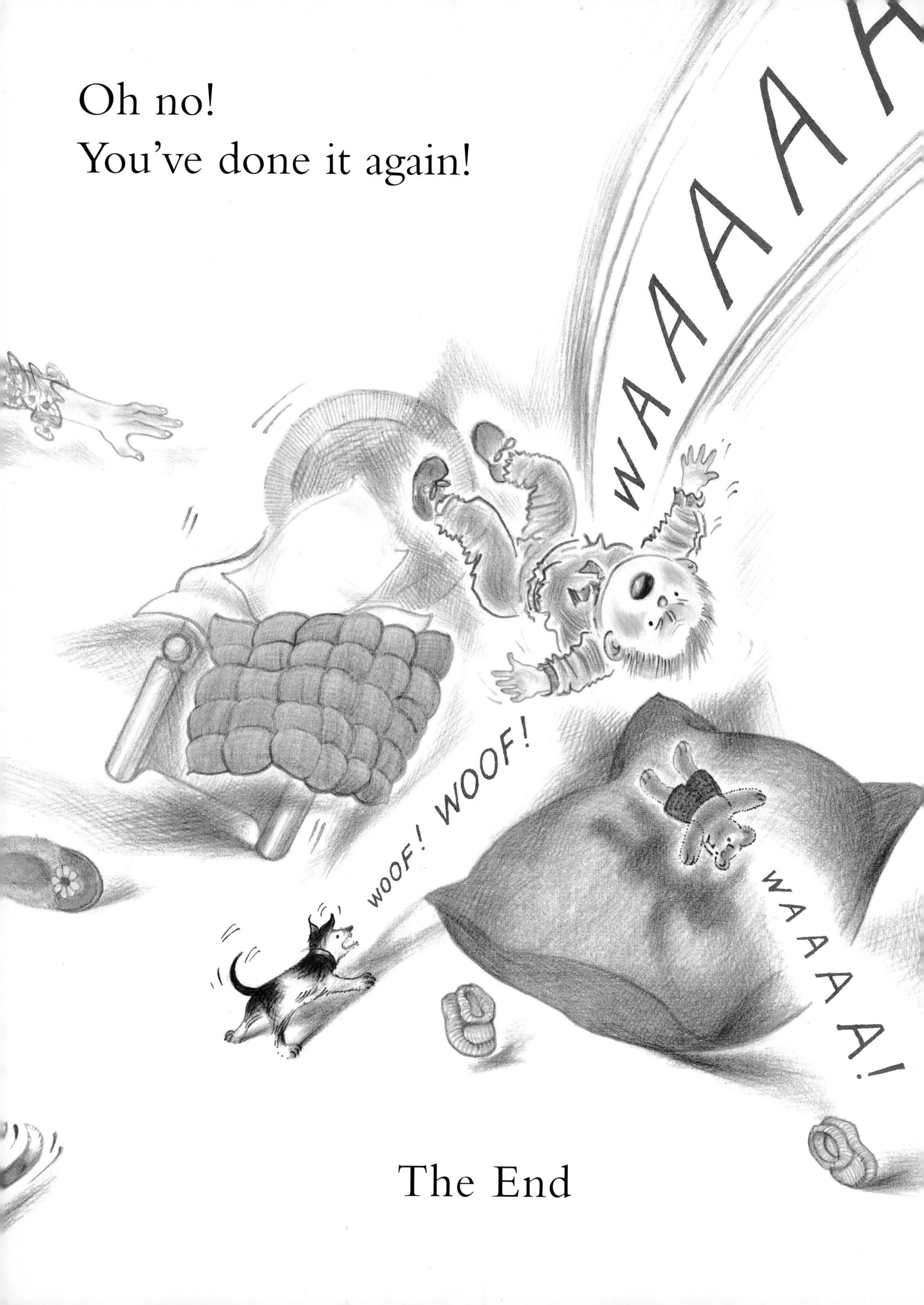

The End